# The WØRST of the VIKINGS

Margaret McAllister

Illustrated by Scoular Anderson

OXFORD
UNIVERSITY PRESS

# OXFORD

UNIVERSITY PRESS

Great Clarendon Street, Oxford OX2 6DP

Oxford University Press is a department of the University of Oxford. It furthers the University's objective of excellence in research, scholarship, and education by publishing worldwide in

*Oxford  New York*

*Athens  Auckland  Bangkok  Bogotá  Buenos Aires  Cape Town*
*Chennai  Dar es Salaam  Delhi  Florence  Hong Kong  Istanbul  Karachi*
*Kolkata  Kuala Lumpur  Madrid  Melbourne  Mexico City  Mumbai  Nairobi*
*Paris  São Paulo  Shanghai  Singapore  Taipei  Tokyo  Toronto  Warsaw*

with associated companies in  *Berlin  Ibadan*

Oxford is a registered trade mark of Oxford University Press in the UK and in certain other countries

ISBN 0 19 919264 2

This book is for all my friends from Viking lands, including all the Scandinavians who came to Alnwick Music Festival. Especially, my love and thanks go to the Synnes and Mollestad families.

Very
Cold

Northumberland
(England)

Home
of the
Vikings

Edwinsbay

End of the
World

Boat
Cave

Ingy's Bay

Dunes

4

# 1

# *The anger of Harald Hairyhand*

By the late white sun of a winter afternoon,
three Viking warriors gazed across the sea.
Tangled hair stuck out wildly from beneath
their helmets. Behind them, on the cliff top,
bitter black smoke filled the sky.

Were they gazing in triumph towards their
homeland?

No. Not these three. They were in disgrace.

The tallest, whose name was Torpid, was
almost asleep. The others who were, in order

of height, Vapid and Morbid, were wondering what would happen when the Viking leader caught up with them.

But to tell you how they came to be in trouble we have to go back to the early morning, when their longships were speeding across the sea.

In the prow of the leading ship stood their chief. His hair and beard were fair as a cornfield, his blue eyes were fierce, and his sword was in his hand. He was Harald Hairyhand. He was leading his men across the North Sea to ransack villages, take the animals, and carry great riches home to Norway.

At one time, men used to call him Harald Stubbylegs because he was the only Viking who had to stand on tiptoe to kiss his granny. But he had grown into a strong man and a powerful fighter, and the last man to call him 'Harald Stubbylegs' never spoke again. (Though some people thought that he was saying 'sorry' as his severed head bounded across the ground.) Now he was the great Harald Hairyhand. From his yellow hair and beard to the toes of his enormous boots, (he wore very thick boots to make himself taller), he was feared more than all other Vikings – except one.

The sweating fair-haired men pulling the oars could see a beach and a cliff top, with a huddle of small wooden buildings. Goats, sheep and cattle grazed nearby.

'Looks sort of nice, doesn't it?' said Vapid.

'Stop your noise at the back of the boat, or I'll feed your guts to the gulls!' roared Harald.

'When we reach the shore, we climb up to the village quickly and quietly. Take them by surprise. Anyone you meet will run before you – if they don't, hack them to pieces. Drive the animals down to the beach. Steal anything worth having.'

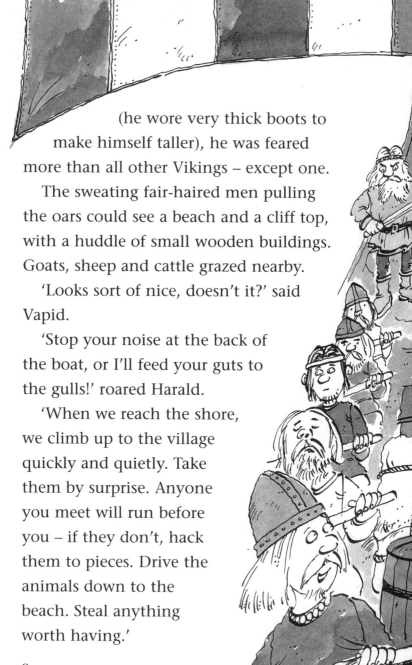

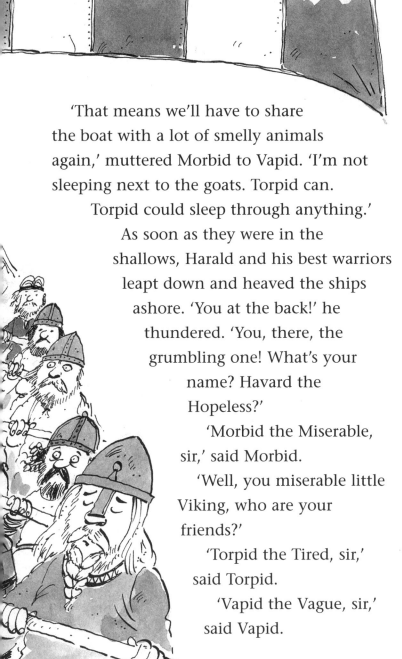

'That means we'll have to share
the boat with a lot of smelly animals
again,' muttered Morbid to Vapid. 'I'm not
sleeping next to the goats. Torpid can.
Torpid could sleep through anything.'
As soon as they were in the
shallows, Harald and his best warriors
leapt down and heaved the ships
ashore. 'You at the back!' he
thundered. 'You, there, the
grumbling one! What's your
name? Havard the
Hopeless?'
'Morbid the Miserable,
sir,' said Morbid.
'Well, you miserable little
Viking, who are your
friends?'
'Torpid the Tired, sir,'
said Torpid.
'Vapid the Vague, sir,'
said Vapid.

9

'Oh,' said Harald, 'the dozy one and the dithery one. You three take the quickest path up the cliffs – the path to the left, can you see it, idiots? That means you get there first, you lucky Vikings! So if anyone is guarding that end of this pathetic village, who gets killed?'

'We do, sir,' said Morbid.

'Now, Vikings,' roared Harald, 'follow me! Fire! Plunder! Pillage! Slaughter!'

Morbid, Torpid and Vapid trudged up the path. The other warriors ran for the steeper, slower climb up the cliffs.

'I hate slaughtering,' said Morbid. 'I'd

rather be on deck-scrubbing duty, but I always get slaughtering.'

'I'm too tired to pillage,' yawned Torpid. 'All that rowing wears you out.'

'I've never been quite sure what pillage is,' said Vapid. 'It's sort of stealing, isn't it? We'll be in trouble if we don't join in. We'd better just pillage a little bit.'

Nobody was guarding the village. Torpid, Vapid and Morbid looked around and wondered how they could plunder, pillage and slaughter without causing too much trouble. The other Vikings were still swarming up the cliffs with drawn swords when Vapid saw a brown and white goat grazing nearby. A loose tethering rope was round its neck.

'I suppose we could sort of steal the goat,' he suggested. 'Is that pillage?'

'It'll bite,' said Morbid.

The Viking warriors had arrived in the village now, roaring with the rage of battle. The villagers screamed and ran and the animals stampeded, horses whinnying in distress.

'Move yourselves, or I'll tear you apart!' roared Harald as he ran past.

'We'd better get out of his way,' said Morbid. 'Is anywhere safe?'

They were near the largest building in the village, which was the only one made of

stone. At least it wouldn't burn down. They slipped inside, Vapid leading the goat. Torpid shut the door to keep the noise out.

'It's dark,' said Morbid. 'Can't see if there's anything worth plundering.'

As their eyes became used to the darkness, they could make out a cross-shaped thing gleaming at the other end of the building, and something in front of it. It might have been a small treasure box.

'At least there's nobody here to kill,' said Torpid. 'What about that cross thing, is it gold? We could plunder that, if it isn't too heavy.'

'I'm interested in the box thing,' said Vapid, and they went to take a better look. 'The flattish, square-ish thing.'

Morbid pulled it towards him. It was brightly painted. Something shone gently in the dark.

'Jewels!' said Torpid. 'Careful how you lift it up, it's falling apart.'

'Typical,' grumbled Morbid. 'Things always

fall apart for me.' But what looked to him like a box falling apart was, in fact, a book. Morbid had heard of books, but never seen one. He carried it to a tiny window and turned the pages very, very gently, because he was afraid of breaking something.

None of them spoke. Nothing they had seen, on sea, on land, in battle or at peace had prepared them for anything so wonderful. They had not dreamed of such patterns, such colours, such delicate twists of scarlet and purple, blue and gold. They gazed at the book as if they were soaking up its colour and craftsmanship. Those gold edgings and the neat rows of black patterns must surely mean something, if only they understood it. In the margins were skilful drawings of birds with

long, intertwined bodies and fierce beaks.
There was a cat, a lion, a man with wings. An
eagle. Swirls, circles and spirals, curls and
whirls, were so bright that the colours could
have been alive and singing.

The pealing of a bell crashed into the
silence. They all jumped, shrieked and
reached for their swords, wildly looking
around, up and down. Where was the
enemy?

'Blooming goat!' growled Morbid.

The goat had wandered off and found the
bell rope. He was chewing hard at it with
determined little tugs. By the time the three
of them had hauled the bell rope from the
goat and the goat from the bell rope, the

clanging was deafening. When it stopped, they heard shouts, the blowing of horns and the clash of weapons, louder and louder. Everybody for miles around must have heard that bell.

'Oops,' said Morbid. 'We've woken up the opposition.'

'I don't think we should have done that,' said Vapid.

'Sometimes, it's best not to wake up in the mornings at all,' sighed Torpid. 'Now what do we do?'

'Er . . . we could . . . sort of . . .' began Vapid.

'Pillage and run?' said Morbid. He stuffed the book down the front of his tunic, and they grabbed the cross and a couple of candlesticks.

'That'll do,' said Torpid, who thought that the real trouble with plundering was carrying all that heavy plunder back to the longships. 'Let's see if we can get this lot down to the beach without having to kill anyone.'

They scuttled to the door, Vapid leading the goat. Morbid gave the church door a hefty shove and tripped over his feet as it was opened from outside by a strong hand.

A hairy hand. Harald's hairy hand, holding his battleaxe.

'If I find who rang that bell I'll slit him end to end and nail him to the door!' roared Harald, as the cries and clashes of battle shook the air. 'The whole country is streaming in to help this village! Who rang that bell?'

Morbid grumbled and Torpid shuffled and

they both stammered that it was nothing to do with them.

They might have got away with it if Vapid hadn't appeared at that moment with the goat, which had chewed right through the rope and brought the rest of it with him for second helpings. The Vikings, stuttering and trembling as they handed over the cross and candlesticks, were terrified of Harald, but the goat wasn't. It stared him out with its long, lazy eyes, chewing steadily. A tassel stuck out from the corner of its mouth.

'That's a *bell* rope!' roared Harald, and swung his battleaxe.

'No, just any old rope,' dithered Vapid. With the side of his axe, Harald walloped the bottom of each Viking in turn.

'You – hopeless – imbeciles!' he yelled, with a wallop for every word. 'You've done enough damage for one day! Get back to the boats and stay there, and take that goat! And,' he called after them as they ran, clutching their bottoms, for the shore, 'after

all this, I might eat you! Or I might just peg
you down on the beach and leave you for the
crows!'

They ran from the village, where armed
men who had heard the ringing of the bell
were charging down from every side to fight
off the Vikings. Hand to hand and sword to
sword they struggled as Torpid, Vapid and

Morbid ran to the beach. They looked out to sea. Home was a long way away.

'Will he really feed us to the crows?' said Morbid. 'He's angry enough.'

They tried to think of a way of escaping and Vapid suggested stealing a longship, but Morbid pointed out that it took a whole crew of Vikings to row one.

'He can't leave us to the crows,' said Vapid. 'There aren't any. Only those little fat things that waddle about.'

'Babies?' said Torpid.

'No, puffins,' said Vapid. 'They look

friendly. I don't suppose they'll eat us, not if they're friendly.'

'They will if they're hungry,' said Morbid, then nobody said anything until it started to rain.

They looked nervously at each other, then over their shoulders. At that moment, Harald Hairyhand was too busy fighting to notice if they disobeyed orders.

They shuffled along the beach and, as the tide was out, were able to walk around the jutting cliffs to a sheltered little bay. There was a cave there, cold and dark, but at least it was dry. Huddling inside, they all saw the same thing.

A boat! It was small enough to row, but big enough to carry them all. It had been left at the back of the cave, with the oars in it.

'Nice boat,' said Torpid.

'Nice bit of pillage,' said Vapid. 'Stealing a boat is sort of pillage, isn't it?'

'Not if we steal it for ourselves,' said Morbid. 'It's only pillage if we steal it for Harald.' They all knew that they had no intention of handing over anything to Harald. Certainly not a boat. And not themselves, either. Together they pushed it to the water's edge.

'Can we keep the goat?' asked Vapid. 'It might, you know, be useful. It's rather a nice goat.'

But the goat did not want to get into that boat. They pushed it and pulled it, but it stood still. They picked it up and stood it in the boat, and it climbed out again. They tried one more time. It kicked Morbid, butted Torpid, and ran away.

'Jump in,' said Torpid. 'We'll have to go without it.'

'I always get wetter than anyone else,' grumbled Morbid as they pushed the boat into the water and climbed in. They saw the goat trotting carelessly across the sand – then a bellow thundered through the air.

'YOU FOUL SCUM! TRAITORS! DESERTERS!'

'That wasn't the goat talking, was it?' asked Vapid.

Above them, on a cliff top, the short and powerful figure of Harald Hairyhand stood like a figurehead. He raised his spear and, with a roar of fury, hurled it at the boat. All three Vikings flung themselves down as the spear skimmed over them and landed in the water.

Morbid fished it out.

'May as well keep it,' he said. 'Don't suppose it'll be any use, but it's a pity to waste it. Now, where are we going?'

'To sleep,' said Torpid, and did.

'Thataway,' said Vapid, pointing away from the burning village. He didn't care where they went, so long as it was away from Harald.

'Yes, but where's "thataway"? Where's the nearest land?'

'Um . . . um . . . er . . . Morbid, do you know these waters at all?'

There was no sound but the dip and slosh of the oars, and a gentle snore. Then Morbid said,

'You don't know where we're going, do you?'

'Sort of no. Do you?'

Dip, slosh, went the oars. Dip, slosh.

'Don't suppose we've got any food and fresh water?' said Morbid.

After digging about in the leather pouches

they carried they found dry bread, a drinking flask half full of ale, and one piece of very hard cheese. It had been there for a long time, and smelt of feet.

'That should keep us going for . . . er . . .' said Vapid.

'Not very long,' said Morbid.

*Torpid lay on a hillside in the sunshine, with music playing nearby. The harvest was in, and beautiful Viking girls sat braiding each other's hair and whispering. Then the prettiest of them, with flowers in her hair, took a jug of ale and walked towards him, smiling. She held out the jug and emptied it over him.*

Torpid woke from his dream, and leapt to his feet.

'I'm wet!' he yelled. Then the boat rocked, and he remembered where he was. 'This boat leaks!'

## 2

# *Lost in the mist*

'We should have known,' grumbled Morbid. He took off his helmet and jammed it over the leak. 'That's why this boat was left alone in that cave, with the oars in. It was waiting to be repaired. Hand over your tunic, Vapid, it's leaking round the edge of my helmet.'

'Does it, er, have to be *my* tunic?' asked Vapid.

'It won't help,' yawned Torpid. 'It'll be soaked through in no time. Where's Harald's spear?'

They plugged the leak by ramming the spear point into the hole. There was still a small puddle seeping very slowly around it, but they baled that out with their helmets.

It grew dark. They took turns to hold the spear in the hole and bale out. They ate and drank a little of their rations, then decided that they had to make the food last, and put the rest away. Then they got it out again and ate a bit more, but they were still hungry. They took turns to keep watch through the night, and even Torpid agreed to stay awake for as long as he could – but after a day and a night, when the food was finished and the drink nearly finished, they were all asleep.

Vapid woke, shivering, stiff, and very cold. He stood up, swaying with the movement of the boat. It was still dark but he could see the water was shallow, so he stepped out and pulled the boat up the beach as far as he could. He wanted to wake the others and tell them they'd reached land, but they had been so tired, and were so fast asleep, that he left them. From the rising of the sun behind him, he knew he was facing west. (He should have worked out that he was in the same country as before but a long way further down the coast, but he'd never been clear about directions.)

He was clear about something else, though. He was hungry, and there wasn't a thing in sight to eat.

High cliffs and sand dunes were all around, but there were winding footpaths through the dunes and a narrow pass through the cliffs. Taking the spear he headed for the right-hand path, changed his mind and turned left, then thought again and went for

the middle, straight across the sand dunes. If he had thought of the dangers of exploring a strange place alone, he wouldn't have done it, but in his hurry to find something to eat he was soon over the dunes and out of sight of the beach.

The sun was rising as Morbid sat up and saw that they had beached. He kicked Torpid to wake him and kicked him again to wake him up properly this time, because he'd gone straight back to sleep.

'Vapid's gone,' said Morbid, looking round. 'He's sure to get lost, so we'll have to find him. We'll probably get eaten by wild animals or taken prisoner, but I suppose we should try. You take the right-hand path through the sand dunes, and I'll go by the cliffs on the left. Meet you back here when the sun's overhead. Got it?'

Torpid yawned and stumbled to the sand dunes. He started singing to wake himself up, and because he liked singing. Morbid stumped off to the cliffs. But by the time the sun was overhead, Torpid had stopped for a rest and fallen asleep again, and Morbid was lost.

The mist was swirling in from the sea, wrapping thin grey cloud about Vapid as he walked further and further over the dunes and down into a valley. It reached the valley before him, and the more he walked, the more he sank into grey mist. He could see only a few metres ahead, and then hardly at all.

'Never mind,' he thought, 'I never knew where I was going in the first place, so I'm no worse off.' Then he heard a woman scream.

He reached for his sword, couldn't find it, and remembered Harald's spear. Spear in hand he ran towards the scream, knowing that he should shout something, and not sure what, but he remembered what Harald used to shout – 'Plunder! Pillage! Slaughter!' – and he yelled it with all his strength.

Dimly he could see a shape ahead of him, becoming clearer with every step. There was a woman, in a homespun tunic that was splattered with something deep red – it was on her hands, too, and on the cauldron in

front of her, and dripped from the hefty stick she held in both hands. She glared with rage.

'Come one step closer and I'll do the plundering and the pillaging and the slaughtering!' she snarled as she brandished the reddened stick.

'Er – sorry.' Vapid backed away. 'Um – good morning – um – I thought you screamed. I was coming to help. But, as you're all right, I'll go. Nice to meet you.'

'Oh, don't worry about the scream, love,' she said. She smiled, put down the stick, and rubbed her red hands on her tunic. 'I just lost my temper with this useless dye, and when I dropped the cauldron on my foot, it was enough to make a saint shout.'

'Oh!' said Vapid. 'Dye?'

'Dye, yes,' she said. 'I make a lot of that. Dye for cloth and paint for decoration and books and that. Come in, if you like, and if you promise not to do any pillaging and slaughtering.'

Morbid went on trudging between the cliffs. He, too, was hampered by the mist. 'I may as well keep going,' he muttered. 'I expect I'll find armies on one side, dragons on the other and a sheer drop in front of me, but I may as well go on.' So he went on, and walked into a wall.

He staggered back muttering curses as his brain spun inside his head. As the dizziness cleared and his eyes stopped watering, he heard a voice.

'Narrow is the gate, and few are those that find it. You missed, brother. Come this way.'

Hand on battleaxe, he followed the voice and walked into a smoky darkness that made him blink and screw up his eyes until he became used to it. The smoke came from a small fire of sticks and sea coal, and by its glow he saw an old man with a white beard.

'Bless you,' said the old man. Morbid didn't know what that meant, but the old man spoke gently and carried no weapons, so he supposed it wasn't anything unpleasant. He crouched to warm himself over the fire, and the old man brought him bread and water. So Morbid ate, keeping his hand on his battleaxe, and watched the firelight dancing on the walls.

There were patterns on those walls, and they reminded him of something. He went to look more closely, tracing the shapes with his finger. The feeling that he was being watched made him turn, and he saw the old man behind him.

'What do these squiggles mean?' asked Morbid.

Far away, Torpid woke up in a shady wood. From somewhere came music and Torpid sat up, wide awake and listening.

The music stopped. A voice called, 'Who are you?'

'Torpid,' he called, looking round. 'Torpid the Tired.'

He heard somebody laugh, but it was a pleasant laugh. A red-haired young man, with a harp in one hand, came out of the wood.

'I'm the Bard,' he said. 'I'm practising this tune but I haven't got it right yet.'

The young Bard played, and Torpid

listened to every note. He had heard harp
music before, but never like this. It was like
listening to the world waking up, or to the
best day of your life, or magic. The Bard
finished his song, and held out the harp to
Torpid.

'It won't bite,' he said. 'Try it.'

Nervously, Torpid took the small harp. He
ran his fingers over the strings and the sound

made him think of bells, and the sea. 'I did that!' he exclaimed.

The Bard laughed. 'I'll teach you to play,' he said. 'But now, I have to go and play to the Hermit. Come with me, if you like.'

# 3

## *Colours and a cave*

Vapid turned round and round, dizzy with colour. Brilliant blue and green, red as bright as jewels, the yellow of sunshine and buttercups, and purple deep as mystery were in vats and jars around him.

'Mind that purple,' called the woman. 'It's hard to get, and expensive.'

Vapid had never really looked at colours before. He had always thought of them as 'a bit like sunset' or 'muddyish'. Now he saw bowls of every shade of yellow from cream to golden, every blue from pale sky to midnight, and every red from sea shell pink to deepest blood.

'Do you use these all yourself?' he asked. Secretly he was longing to paint a pot or dye a garment, or anything that would give him a chance to play with the colours. 'Do you dye cloth?'

'I do, yes,' she said, 'but the little paints are for the books. The old Hermit in the cave, he does the books. If he lived in a monastery he'd have somebody there to make his paint. As it is, he sits in his cave and I send him his colours. The Vikings burned his monastery.' She looked closely at his helmet. 'Speaking of Vikings, what's that on your head?'

Vapid whipped off the helmet, fidgeted with it, and held it out. 'It's for you,' he said. 'You can use it for a paint pot.'

'Funny paint pot,' she muttered. 'It'll fall over.' But when she had embedded it in the earth, it looked as if it could be useful.

'I suppose I should go,' said Vapid, though he looked longingly at the paints. 'I don't know where my friends are.'

'Where did you leave them?'

'Somewhere on the beach.' He turned to face her, and wondered where he had put down the spear, and why she had picked it up. She looked tremendously strong.

He backed away as she advanced towards him, pointing the spear and, staggering backwards in fear, he tripped over a stone. With a long, fierce stride she was upon him. But before he could move, she had taken his hand and pulled him to his feet.

'I only want

you to hold this,' she said, 'while I get my bits and pieces together.' She took a well-loaded basket which she strapped to her back, and filled another with small pots of paint. She gave this one to Vapid, keeping hold of the spear as she did so.

'We'll take this lot to the Hermit first,' she said. 'By the way, my name's Ingy.'

'I'm Vapid.'

'I thought so. I like this spear,' she said, and used it as a walking stick. 'Take care, don't drop that paint.'

Torpid followed the Bard to the Hermit's cave and wondered how much further it could be. It was hard work to keep up, and he was hungry. A rest and something to eat would be good, only he didn't like to ask. He stopped for an enormous yawn.

'I'm sorry!' called the Bard. 'Shall we sing? Singing always makes the way seem easier.'

Torpid liked singing, and was good at it, but the Viking songs were all about hacking people to bits and hanging their heads from

your horse's saddle and splattering blood all over your nice new longship, so he didn't think he should sing one of those. The Bard began a song all about mountains and rivers and heaven and earth and living creatures, and they walked uphill along a path that twisted and narrowed, and then . . .
and then they saw two men sitting at a cave entrance. Their heads were bent,

and they seemed to be drawing with their fingers on the ground. Torpid recognized one of them.

A sound of slithering, a cry of 'help!' and a hail of loose stones made them all look up. Vapid and Ingy were stumbling and slithering down a cliff path, and Vapid was carrying something in a basket.

'Morbid! Torpid!' he called, with a broad smile.

'Vapid! Morbid!' called Torpid, waving.

Morbid looked up. 'Oh, it's you two,' he said, and went back to his drawing.

# 4

# *Ingy the Thingy*

'And they shall come from afar bearing gifts,' said the bearded old man. He stood up stiffly to welcome his visitors.

'Good morning, Hermit,' said Ingy. 'Put the basket in the cave, Vapid, and come and sit down. We'll eat soon.'

At the word 'eat', everyone brightened up, even Morbid. Soon they were all seated outside the cave in a circle. Vapid tried to explain that they were, um, sort of warriors, but they weren't very, um, good at it, and they just, sort of, turned up here, but Ingy stopped him.

'Eat now, talk later,' she said. She undid the basket from her back and brought out bread, butter, cheese, cold meat, cold chicken, smoked fish, apples and jars of ale, and after that nobody said much until they had finished.

'Now,' said Ingy, 'the Hermit lives in a cave and makes books. The Bard lives anywhere, and makes music. I live on the edge of the village – I have to – some of those dyes smell foul in summer.'

'She's the most important person around here,' smiled Bard. 'She's the Helper.'

'The Wise One,' said the Hermit.

'The Thingy,' said Ingy firmly. 'Just the Thingy. Now, what are we to do with you? You can stay here, if you make yourselves useful.'

'Can I help you?' said Vapid eagerly. 'I could, er, mix things, or fetch things, or . . .'

'Fall into things,' muttered Morbid.

'You can learn to make colours,' said Ingy. 'Maybe to use them, too.'

'It's no good asking Torpid, he's asleep again,' said the Bard. 'But I think he wants to learn music.'

'That leaves me,' said Morbid gruffly. 'I know what I want. I don't suppose you'll let me do it, but I'll tell you.'

He reached down and drew a zigzag on the ground. 'D'you see that? That's M for Morbid, that is! I've just learned that! I want to do what the Hermit does. I want to read and write.'

The Hermit smiled a deep smile that he couldn't hide behind his beard.

'My son, listen to the words of instruction,' he said. 'It's a long time since I had a pupil. One day, you might help me to make books.'

'Books?' Morbid suddenly peered down inside his tunic.

'Has he got a ferret down there?' asked Ingy, but Morbid wasn't listening. With great care he lifted out the treasure they had taken from the church.

'That's a book, isn't it?' he said. 'First one I've ever seen.'

The Hermit's face was as bright as if he saw a vision. Joy and pain glowed in his eyes. His old hands trembled as he took the book and, slowly and lovingly, turned its pages.

'Can you read it?' said Morbid eagerly.

'Read it? Read it?' He gave a cry that was half a laugh and half a sob. 'I wrote it!'

'You'd better have it back then,' said Morbid. It wasn't an easy thing to say, but he knew he had to.

'I didn't make it for myself,' said the Hermit. 'I made it for the church at Edwinsbay. Now, I wonder how it came to be hidden down a man's tunic? A man who wears a helmet, and carries a sword and battleaxe?'

Morbid would have lied but the Hermit wasn't a person he wanted to lie to, so he and Vapid told their story. Morbid told it the short way and Vapid told it the long way and Torpid snored.

'We never wanted to plunder,' said Vapid. 'We only kept that book, and Harald might have burned it if we hadn't hidden it. Oh, and we stole a goat, but I don't know what happened to that. I expect Harald took it.'

'He's probably eaten it by now,' grunted Morbid. 'I liked that goat. It had a nice face.'

'Well, if you're so useless as Vikings you'd better stay here,' said Ingy. 'Come on, then, work! Morbid, get to your reading. Vapid, come with me, and Torpid – oh, can't somebody wake him up?'

So they stayed. They stayed all winter, and into the next spring. Morbid worked hard and learned to read all the stories in the book. He became almost happy, and the Hermit said he couldn't be 'the Miserable' any more.

Torpid learned to play the harp, sing, and

stay awake, all at the same time. He learned the power of a lively tune to stir people up, and a gentle one to bring peace. He learned sad songs that would make you cry, funny ones to make you laugh, and stirring ones to make you bold. The Bard said he was a natural musician and should have been making music all his life.

Vapid, under Ingy's instruction, found that he couldn't be vague about paint. It was no good saying something was 'not quite red', or 'sort of blue'. He had to know his scarlet from his crimson, his indigo from his purple, his egg yolk yellow from his butter yellow. When he took paint to the cave the Hermit would cut him a pen, and he would draw patterns and pictures. He liked that best of all. Sometimes they all forgot they had ever been failed Vikings in longships. It was as if they had always lived with these peaceful people. The spear came in useful for stirring paint, and for playing games on the beach, but nobody ever did any harm with it.

One spring afternoon, when the day's work
was finished, the Vikings and Ingy were
playing spear-throwing games on the beach.
Ingy, who had a powerful arm, was doing
extremely well, when Torpid pointed out to
sea and said, 'What's that?'

A small boat was approaching, very slowly.
It was still far away, but it looked very like
the boat they had arrived in. Three of them
had taken turns to row that boat, but in this
one, there was one man. He rowed wearily, as
if he had been at sea for a long, long time.

# 5

## The story of the stranger

As the boat drew near, they could see the rower. His helmet looked very much like a Viking helmet, and there was something familiar about him. Morbid and Vapid waded out to pull the little boat to shore, while Ingy and Torpid set about making a fire because, Ingy said, their visitor would be cold.

The man in the boat was so stiff and chilled they had to take an arm each and heave him out, and he walked rolling from side to side as if he were still at sea. In spite of his helmet, he couldn't be a real Viking. His hair was too short, and so was he. He was beardless, with a dimpled chin.

As they gradually let him go, the stranger managed to stay upright and not fall over. But when he turned to shake the hands of his rescuers, his face turned to horror and fury. As he looked up at Vapid, then Morbid, then

Torpid, his face darkened and twitched with rage.

'YOU THREE!' he bellowed. 'I SWEAR I WILL MURDER YOU ALL AND SPREAD YOUR ENTRAILS ON THE SAND! EVERYTHING IS YOUR FAULT, YOU IMBECILES!'

'Oh. Hello, Harald,' said Vapid. 'I didn't recognize you without . . .'

Harald Hairyhand's sword was already in his hand, and it was too late to remember that none of them carried weapons any more. The blade flashed as he lunged at Torpid. There was a grunt and a thump as Morbid dived at Harald's ankles and toppled him, and Ingy forced him to let go of the sword by tickling him in the armpits. Harald kicked, struggled, threatened and cursed, but there were four of them to hold him down – three, when Ingy offered Harald a drink from a leather bottle and some food from the basket. By the time he'd eaten two loaves of bread, a whole chicken, a cheese, a smoked fish, and one more loaf to finish off with, and Torpid had played some soothing music, he was in a slightly better mood. At least he looked as if he wouldn't kill anyone just yet.

'The new look suits you,' said Torpid. 'Short hair and no beard.' A stone spun through the air, and only missed him because he ducked.

'It is NOT a look!' snarled Harald. 'I spent years growing that beard.' He stopped to lick chicken grease from his fingers, then told his story.

'When you feeble runts raided the church and woke the whole countryside, we had war on our hands. I could have raided the whole coastline if it wasn't for that, but their reinforcements came from everywhere at once. We ended up on the beach, surrounded on three sides, outnumbered ten to one. The only way we could go was back to the longships.'

'Why didn't you get into them, then?' asked Morbid. 'You could have gone home.' He ducked as Harald aimed the next pebble at him.

'That's what they all said,' snarled Harald, 'but I hadn't come all that way for nothing! How would it look when I got home? When Fetid the Foul went raiding, he brought back half a village and a dozen prize boars. And what about Rancid the Rotten?'

Rancid the Rotten was the one Viking who was even more feared than Harald. At the mention of his name, all the Vikings shuddered.

'Rancid,' went on Harald, 'carried off enough gold and silver to sink a dragon. On my last expedition, you could have suffocated a troll with the gold I brought home! This time, what did I have?'

'A goat,' said Vapid helpfully. Harald threw another pebble and everyone ducked except Ingy, who caught it.

'Stop that,' she said. 'You'll do somebody a mischief. So you wanted to gather your men for one more attack, did you?'

'I kept them on the beach that night, ready to attack at dawn. I was on duty for the first watch, then I slept until morning, and when I woke up . . .'

He was looking at the sand. The faintest shade of pink had crept into the smooth face.

'It wasn't the goat's fault,' he muttered. 'It's a nice goat, and it was hungry. When I woke up, it had eaten my beard. And most of my hair. I'd been growing that beard since I was fourteen. Even Rancid the Rotten was impressed by that beard. And not a whisker was left, and there was the goat, with half my pony-tail hanging out of its mouth, and all my men laughing! Do you hear? LAUGHING AT ME!'

'That's really sad,' said Morbid, trying not to look at Vapid.

'Terribly sad,' giggled Vapid, and Torpid couldn't say anything because he was rolling on the sand laughing and stuffing his fist in his mouth.

'They wouldn't listen to a word I said, after that,' said Harald. 'They weren't going to obey me, looking like this. They were rowing

back to Norway before you could say
"puffins".'

'Didn't they let you go with them?' asked
Ingy.

'Do you think I was going to go with them? I had my pride. I stayed on that beach, and when the locals arrived I made the best fight of it I could. You should have seen that fight! Soaked was the sand, and smeared with scarlet . . .'

'Oh, don't start,' said Morbid. He knew Harald wanted to tell a long and exaggerated story with heaps of alliteration like, 'fighting with fury he felled the foemen', and, 'Proud was his purpose. He panicked the puffins.'

'So, after the fight, what happened?' asked Ingy.

'They took me prisoner,' he sulked. 'I should have died fighting, but they took me prisoner.'

'That must have been rough,' said Morbid. 'A damp, smelly cell underground, rotten food, no blanket, and things crawling over you in the night.'

'I've seen worse prisons,' shrugged Harald. 'It wasn't so bad. In fact . . .' and for the first time he sounded less like a Viking warrior and more like a Norwegian farmer, 'the bread was a bit dry and the blanket was scratchy, but for a dungeon, it was reasonable. They talked about whether they should kill me, but they decided to let me live and repair the damage we'd done. They wouldn't let me grow my hair and beard again, in case I frightened the children.

'I worked hard on the land, and they let me break in horses. I enjoyed it. I used to do all that at home, before my older brother inherited everything and I had to go raiding and pillaging. They're nice people at Edwinsbay, once you stop killing them and get to know them. And, in spite of everything it did, I liked that goat. I looked after him. And he liked me, he followed me everywhere.'

'It was waiting for his beard to grow again,' muttered Morbid, but he made sure Harald didn't hear. Out loud, he only said, 'And then what happened?'

'VIKINGS!' exploded Harald. 'There we

were, a happy, peaceful community minding our own business, and along came all these Viking ships, ready to raid and plunder!'

'Terrible,' agreed Morbid. 'There's some wicked people about.'

'Any, um, particular Vikings?' asked Vapid.

'Rancid,' muttered Harald, to gasps of terror from all round the fire. 'I'm surprised you can't catch a whiff of him from here.'

'They say the smell of Rancid the Rotten can kill a puffin at twenty paces,' shuddered Torpid. 'He's always killing people and never washes his hands afterwards. I've heard it said that his feet are stuck to his sandals.'

'I did my best,' said Harald, 'I fought to save Edwinsbay, but Rancid's men caught me and cast me off to sea in that leaky little tub. The worst of it is that Rancid and his men didn't just raid the village and go. They've taken over, and forced the local people to work for them. They mean to stay.'

At the thought of kind, gentle people ruled over by Rancid the Rotten they sat around in glum silence. All except Ingy, who stomped across the sand and came back, dragging a boat from a cave.

'Good thing I mended it,' she said.

'Haven't I seen that boat thing before?' said Vapid.

'It's ours!' said Torpid. 'We rowed all the way here in that.'

'Who did?' muttered Morbid. 'You were asleep.'

'Sorry, I don't understand this,' said Vapid. 'Have I missed something? Why

do we need the boat again?'

'Because,' explained Harald, 'we're not going to leave Rancid the Rotten treating all those people like slaves, are we, troll-face? We have to go there and throw out Rancid and his men. It looks like hard work, but that isn't the point.'

'We'll all get killed,' said Morbid. 'But that isn't the point, either. We have to do it.'

## 6

# *The return of the Vikings*

'We'll arm ourselves before we go,' said Harald. 'Swords and battleaxes.'

'You won't need them,' said Ingy. 'You can have this old spear if you like.' Harald took the spear and inspected it.

'This was a fine spear until I threw it at you lot,' he said. 'It's blunt now. Four of us, and a blunt spear, to take on Rancid the Rotten and all his Vikings. And you're all useless fighters.'

'Who said anything about fighting?' said Ingy.

Morbid scowled. 'Rancid won't go just because we ask him nicely,' he said.

'Yes, but there's only four of you and three of you are no good at fighting,' said Ingy. 'What do you think your brains are for?'

They said a quick, sad and difficult goodbye to the Hermit, the Bard and Ingy.

Vapid had some dyes to take with him, and Torpid had his own harp and his whistle, and Morbid had a quill and ink and a bit of parchment. To his great joy the Hermit gave him the book, saying that it came from Edwinsbay and it should be returned there.

At last, Ingy shoved the boat out. It bobbed and rocked, and they were on their way. Then Vapid remembered that he had left his helmet upside down full of orange dye, but it was too late to go back.

*Torpid raised his sword two-handed over the cowering figure of Rancid the Rotten and with all his strength crashed it down on his enemy. The sword in his hands turned into a puffin which twisted round to look at him, and Rancid sprang up with a wet fish in each hand . . .*

Torpid, as usual, was dreaming. He woke as Morbid sloshed water in his face.

'Wake up, useless,' Morbid was saying. 'Land in sight.'

Torpid yawned enormously, stretched, and sat up. He was wet and cold and didn't feel much like facing anyone, let alone Rancid.

'This isn't where we landed,' he said.

'Not exactly,' said Vapid.

'Course it isn't,' said Harald. 'We're not steering for the bay. They'll have lookouts everywhere. We're heading for the south side, and the cave where you found the boat in the first place. Then we'll spy out the land and see what we can do.'

'Kill Rancid and all his men and set the people free,' said Morbid. 'Easy peasy, the goat smells cheesy.'

'Rumble mumble, Morbid's a grumble,' sang Torpid.

'I wish I knew what happened to the goat,' said Harald sadly, as they brought the boat into land. 'I called him Eric. I hope Rancid hasn't killed him.'

'Never mind, Harald,' said Torpid as they pulled the boat up the beach. 'We'll find him.'

They heaved the boat into the cave where they had first found it. The sun was high, and Harald suggested they should stay out of the way until evening.

'That's when the Vikings all sit around, get drunk and tell terrific tales about their battles,' he said. 'There are guards on duty,

but they're usually drunk, too, or asleep, or both.'

So they stayed in the cave where Torpid played his harp very quietly, and Morbid opened his book and read stories, and Vapid drew patterns on the ground with a sharp stick and Harald talked about the good times he'd had among these people before Rancid the Rotten came. As the afternoon dragged on they talked less and less, and looked out at the fading light. Torpid played the wrong notes because he couldn't concentrate, Morbid lost the place in his book, and Vapid gave up. At last Harald declared that it was dark enough to creep out and do some spying.

'Can't see a thing,' muttered Vapid.

'Be quiet and remember your Viking training,' said Harald.

They slipped out in single file, and stood back to look at the top of the cliffs. A fire was burning low, glowing darkly as if it was going out, and this, said Harald, was a good sign.

'It means the guards are neglecting it,' he said, 'so they're probably drunk and sleeping it off. I'll climb up there and have a look, and wave if it's safe to come up.'

'No, I'll do it,' said Torpid quickly.

'*You?*' exclaimed Harald. 'But you're . . .'

'Useless, yes, I know,' whispered Torpid. 'So if I get caught, it's no great loss. We need you, Harald, you're the leader.'

'I'll go behind you,'
muttered Morbid, 'in case
you drop off.'

Torpid scanned the cliff
and said that dropping
off was something he'd
rather not think about,
thank you. Harald
protested again, but
Torpid and Morbid were
already scrambling up
the cliff-side, feeling

for foot-holds in the dark, not daring to look down at the moonlit sea.

Step by step, never knowing if the next handhold would be safe, they inched their way up, and slowly, breath by breath and struggle by struggle, they climbed until they hauled themselves over the cliff top where two guards snored by the fire. Far away, they could hear the singing of the Viking troops. It was loud, flat and very bad. Not a single guard was awake. Morbid waved to the others to join them.

'You're still awake!' whispered Vapid in surprise, as Torpid pulled him up.

'This is too exciting to sleep through!' he said. They lay flat on the grass and looked at the huts, the church, the dying guard fires and the pens full of animals.

'Now what?' said Vapid.

'That's Rancid's hut, the biggest one,' whispered Harald. 'The one with the . . .' he stopped. He was staring at something.

'With the what?' asked Torpid.

'The one,' went on Harald, with a tremble in his voice, 'with the goat tied up outside it. And that's not any old goat. It's Eric!'

# 7

## *The revenge of Harald Hairyhand*

Morbid grabbed at Harald's tunic, but it was too late. He was running to the hut where the goat stood tethered. He put his arms round its neck, and it bleated a welcome.

The guards rolled over. One propped himself on his elbow. Torpid, Morbid and Vapid flattened themselves and tried not to breathe. The half-awake guard yawned noisily.

'It's just that goat,' he said.

'What goat?' slurred the other.

'Tomorrow's dinner,' said the first, and rolled back to sleep.

They waited until the steady rumble of snoring told them that the guards were well and truly asleep again. Then they crawled like

snakes to the hut.

There was no goat. And no Harald.

Vapid, still flat on the grass, turned his head enough to whisper, 'Didn't anyone see them go?'

'We were all keeping our heads down,' said Morbid. 'Couldn't see a thing. I should think he's been caught.'

'We would have heard something,' Vapid

pointed out. 'A fight, or a yell. They would have made a noise, like you do when you're getting caught by a Viking.'

From the darkness came a muffled bleat. They all jumped, though they were lying down.

'It came from that way,' said Vapid. 'No, that way . . . no . . .'

'Shut up and listen!' whispered Torpid. The goat bleated again, a sort of muffled complaint as if someone was trying to keep its mouth shut. Then there was silence. It was a long, dark and frightening silence.

When the goat bleated again, it was in Morbid's right ear. It was followed by a quick, sharp whisper from Harald: 'Come behind the hut and be quiet!' Hushed as he was, there was a note of triumph in his voice.

Swiftly they followed him and huddled behind the hut, where the goat tried to bleat and eat Morbid at the same time.

'He's done it!' whispered Harald, with his arms round the goat. 'He's done it!'

'Done what?' yawned Torpid, feeling he'd been awake for too long.

'What he likes doing,' explained Harald. 'I knew he would! I took him in the hut while Rancid was asleep, and he ate his beard! Every scrap, and most of his hair!'

'Oh, good,' said Torpid, and rubbed his eyes.

'Don't you see?' said Harald. 'When he did that to me, my men wouldn't follow me any more. So Rancid's men won't follow him either!'

Vapid and Torpid tried to cheer without making a noise. Morbid shook his head.

'It's not enough,' he said. 'His men might refuse to follow him, but they'll just choose a new leader and stay here. Your men took to the boats and rowed away, but they already wanted to go. Rancid's men don't.'

'Can't we, sort of, *make* them want to go?' said Vapid. 'Scare them off, or something?'

'Vikings don't scare easily,' said Harald.

'I do,' said Vapid, but they ignored him.

'We've got to find something,' said Morbid. 'Something that makes them so terrified they'll go running back to their ships like lemmings.'

Poor Torpid was now fast asleep. Vapid was gazing up at the stars and wondering which ones were which. Harald was a true Viking warrior, but he was short and beardless and didn't look scary. Neither did Morbid.

'Think,' said Morbid. 'Everybody's frightened of something. What are these Vikings frightened of?'

Then Harald and Morbid grinned at each other. They had both thought of an answer.

'Come on, Vapid,' said Harald. 'And wake up Torpid. We need him.'

Dawn came overcast and cold over the village. The cock crowed, coughed, and went back to sleep.

It woke the men and women who faced another day of slavery. It woke the children, who supposed that today would be all work and no play, as usual, and not enough to eat because Rancid's men took most of the food. It woke Rancid the Rotten, who sat up, feeling something was wrong, but not knowing exactly what.

It woke Rancid's Vikings, bleary with sleep and sore-headed from drinking, ready to take out their foul temper on the local people. In the early half-light, they staggered out of their huts.

What they saw and heard made the blood chill in their veins, and the hair prickle like frost on their arms. Every face turned pale.

A song rose into the air. It was a loud, mysterious wail of a song, like a dirge of death or the moaning of the north wind, long, slow, and fearful.

These Vikings never feared any living creature. They feared the dead.

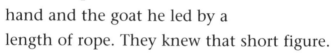

In the grey early morning they saw a figure standing on the raised ground above Rancid's hut. Everything about him was as pale as ashes, his clothes, his face, and even the spear in his hand and the goat he led by a length of rope. They knew that short figure.

They knew the thick boots, the beardless face and the cropped hair. They remembered how Harald Hairyhand was sent away in a small boat. They knew, too, that the goat – the very goat they were to slaughter today – was Harald's goat. They whispered to each other.

'Harald Hairyhand has come back from the sea . . .'

'. . . from the grave . . .'

'He has come for his enemy.'

'He has come for his revenge.'

'He's come for his goat.'

The figure advanced very, very slowly. Rancid's men shuffled back.

At that moment, Rancid the Rotten staggered from his hut, a spear in his hand.

'What are you lot staring at?' he growled. 'Move yourselves, or I'll spear whoever's nearest!'

At the sight of him, another murmur of dismay ran through the terrified Vikings. The terrible spectre on the hill had stolen the beard of Rancid the Rotten.

'It will take all our beards,' someone whispered. They shrank back, step by step.

In the damp morning air, Rancid felt strangely cold. He didn't normally notice a draught around the back of his neck and his chin . . . He put up his hand and found a stubbly, spotty, rather podgy space where his beard had been.

'STOP STARING AT ME!' he bellowed.

'We're not staring at you, sir,' stammered one of his men, pointing a trembling finger.

For the first time, Rancid heard the mournful singing and the bleating of a goat. He turned round.

At the sight of the ghostly figure, the strength soaked out of Rancid as if he were boneless. If he had been alone, he would have turned and run, or hidden under his shield, but he didn't want to look a coward in front of his men.

'To the longships! To the longships!' muttered the Vikings to each other.

'Stay, you idiots!' bawled Rancid. 'You weak, scared, pathetic little puffins! One dead man can't hurt you!'

At any other time, they would have obeyed him, but not now. No leader could protect them from a ghost, especially this nearly bald leader with the spotty chin.

Rancid made one last attempt. He launched his spear at the figure as it walked steadily towards him.

It was a spear throw that would have killed any living man. It hit the spectre, and bounced off. At the sight of the ghost stepping over the spear, still advancing, every single warrior turned and fled to the longships. The villagers let them go. They were closing in around Rancid as he knelt quivering on the ground.

From their shelter behind the hut, Torpid, Vapid and Morbid looked out.

'You can stop wailing now, Torpid,' said Morbid.

'I thought it was rather good,' said Torpid indignantly. 'It's an ancient lament for the dead. Have they all gone yet?'

'Harald's going to stay there until they're well out of the way,' said Vapid. 'What shall we do about Rancid? Do you think we should, sort of, rescue him? I mean, I know he's Rancid the Rotten, but he's a Viking and we're still sort of Vikings.'

'I don't think these villagers'll do him much harm,' said Torpid with a yawn. 'Harald says they're peace-loving people. I don't suppose they'll do anything really nasty to him. Except wash him.'

This, they agreed, was probably the worst thing that could happen to Rancid the Rotten. Torpid complained about being up half the night, and then fell asleep.

When the longships were out of sight, Harald stopped being a ghost and came to join them and wash the lead paint and ashes off his face. 'Well done us!' he said.

'I used up the white lead on his face,' said Vapid. 'But finishing him off with ashes worked rather well.'

'It's a good thing you thought of changing the spears,' said Harald to Morbid. He was carrying Rancid's own spear which he had taken in the night, leaving the blunt one in its place. 'That old one nearly knocked me over, but it didn't do me any harm. I wonder how Rancid's getting on?'

'I'd go and find out,' said Morbid, 'but I still look like a Viking. The villagers might nobble me.'

'Leave it to me,' said Harald. 'I'm their friend.'

Everybody from the village seemed to be hurrying to the beach. Harald ran after them crying out that he was their old friend, Harald Hairyhand, and very much alive. They greeted him with delight as he explained who his friends were and how they had scared away Rancid's Vikings. Torpid, Morbid and Vapid suddenly found themselves lifted

shoulder high, carried down to the beach,
and invited to be honoured guests at The
Washing of Rancid.

As the puffins gathered on the cliff tops to
watch, Rancid was led into the sea and
washed, and washed and washed, until his
clothes finally unstuck themselves from his

body. They scrubbed him until he changed colour, and so did the sea. They washed the lice from his hair and the bugs from his tunic and the grime from between his toes. They washed out the mushrooms growing in his sandals. They washed out the tangles in his chest hair, and a few large caterpillars floated away from behind his ears. When he was as smooth and pink as a bathed baby, they dried him and put him in clean clothes, and he curled up on the sand, biting his nails and whimpering.

'Poor thing,' said Vapid. 'Now what should we do with him?'

'Ingy would know,' said Morbid. 'She'd sort him out.'

'Ingy the Thingy?' said a woman in the crowd. 'You know her, do you?'

It turned out that Ingy was well known to some of the people of Edwinsbay. Several of them offered to take Rancid and hand him over to her. So he was tied up and put in a boat, and taken along the coast to Ingy's Bay.

For the rest of their lives they stayed happily with the people of Edwinsbay. Torpid became their Bard, and Vapid taught them to make dyes and paints, and to use them.

Morbid, of course, returned their book to the church, and he and Vapid went on making books. They all married and had

children and grew to be old, but they went
on with their music and their books and their
pictures to the end of their days.

Harald kept horses and goats and a tame puffin, and was very happy. He became famous as a goat keeper and Eric followed him everywhere, nibbling lovingly at his tunic.

Rancid the Rotten never fully recovered from being washed. He became Ingy's servant, and promised to obey her faithfully so long as he didn't have to wash more than once a year. He was very strong, and made himself useful chopping wood and building houses and strangling wolves with his bare hands.

When Morbid was old, he decided to write down their story in a book. But he was so very old that he sometimes forgot things, and became confused, and didn't always remember events exactly the way they happened. Besides, his handwriting was getting wobbly, and the people who made copies of his book couldn't be sure if they'd got it right.

So that is the story of Morbid, Torpid,

Vapid, and Harald Hairyhand, as Morbid told
it. But is that really how it happened?

What do you think?

# About the Author

This book owes everything to my husband, Tony. Long ago, during a very silly conversation, he invented three people whose names were Torpid, Vapid and Morbid. We agreed that they were Vikings, but not very good ones, and this story grew, very slowly, from there.

Tony and I have spent much of our lives on the North East coast. The nearest to Vikings we ever met are our lovely Norwegian friends. I hope they like this book.

## Other Treetops books at this level include:
*Aliens at Paradise High* by Annie Dalton
*The Mean Dream Wonder Machine* by Margaret McAllister
*Luke Lively and the Castle of Sleep* by Debbie White
*Rat Squad* by Nick Warburton
*Go to the Dragon-maker* by Shirley Isherwood

## Also available in packs:
*Stage 15 pack E*          0 19 919267 7
*Stage 15 class pack E*    0 19 919268 5